To our sweet kids:

CHVN

Ted the Tortoise is shy but
he's learning to come out of his shell,
He loves learning new things and
does it oh so well.

One day his family took him to go see
his very first basketball game,
And he was so amazed by what he saw
that his life would never be the same.

The players dribbled and ran and jumped high in the air!
And they bounced the ball into the net from off the little red square.

They traveled down the court
at lightning-fast speed!
And he could tell that it was so much fun,
that was guaranteed.

Ted was filled with excitement
and suddenly he knew,
That he wanted to be one of
the great basketball players too.

So Ted grabbed an old basketball
and he headed to the park,
Mom said, "don't forget about
dinner honey, be home before dark!"

He was so excited that
he ran the entire way,
He imagined scoring his first basket
and was so excited to play.

He was surprised when he saw
that the court was so full,
And Ted got quite nervous seeing
Gabby the Giraffe and Barry the Bull.

He thought "Maybe I should go back home"
so he headed back down the street,
when he heard "Come play with us, Ted!"
invited Sasha the Sheep.

He thought for a moment after Sasha called his name,
Will Ted come out of his shell and agree to join the game?

Ted suddenly turned around
and he shyly agreed,
He thought if he just did what
the pros do then surely, he'd succeed.

They started the game and
Frank the Fox passed Ted the ball,
But Ted quickly lost his balance
and it suddenly made him fall.

Later in the game Barry the Bull
knocked Ted's glasses
right to the ground,
And Ted landed on the back
of his shell, and he spun
all around.

Ted went back home feeling incredibly sad,
Even though he had never played before,
he didn't think he would be that bad.

Mom later asked "What's wrong, Ted?
You haven't touched your tortellini, your favorite dish!
Know that you can always talk to me
about anything that you wish."

"I thought I could be a basketball player but I am as slow as can be,
I'm just not meant to play basketball and everyone can see."

"You have to practice and practice my dear, that's the only way!
And if you asked the world's greatest players,
that's what all of them would say.

"The more you practice anything, the better that you'll get,
So, give it a little more time, just don't give up yet."

He thought for a moment,
and he knew mom was right!
He decided to go back to the park
the next day at the first sign of light.

When Ted arrived at the court,
he saw Sasha the Sheep and
Frank the Fox, too,

Sasha said "so, you want to learn
how to play, we would both
love to help you!"

Sasha taught Ted how to dribble
and he learned it pretty fast!
He laughed the whole time,
Ted was having a blast.

Frank showed Ted the proper shooting form and it really helped a lot,
And they all jumped for joy when Ted made his first shot.

They practiced altogether
week after week,
And Ted became a wonderful player
with outstanding technique.

One sunny day, everyone met
at the park after school,
Ted was about to play against
Gabby the Giraffe and
Barry the Bull.

He suddenly felt so nervous and
he grew so concerned,
When Sasha Sheep shouted,
"Trust in yourself Ted,
and all that you've learned!"

Ted then thought about
all of his practices
at the rise of the sun,
And how he grew to love
this sport that was
so much fun.

The old Ted would have hidden in his shell
and trembled with fear,
But it was a brand-new tougher Ted
that was standing right here.

His mom was even supporting
from the crowd and cheering on her son,
And in the next moment the game had finally begun.

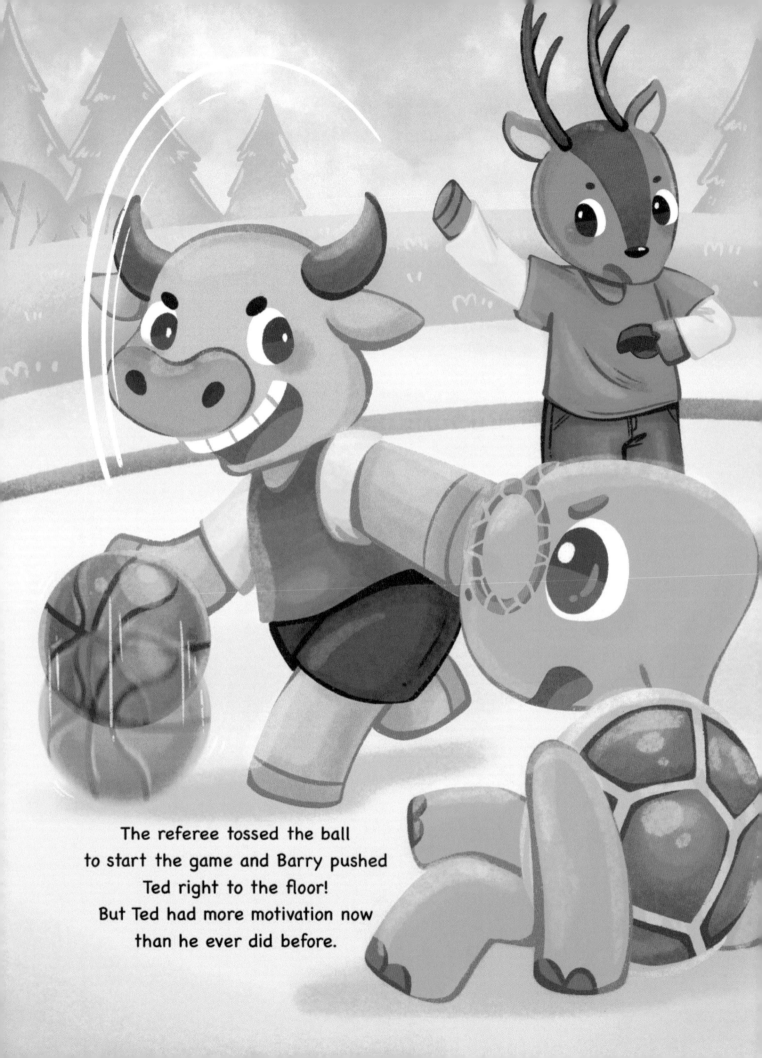

The referee tossed the ball
to start the game and Barry pushed
Ted right to the floor!
But Ted had more motivation now
than he ever did before.

He hopped to his feet and brushed of his shell,
He was focused on the game and everyone could tell.

Ted dribbled the ball to the hoop when
Gabby the Giraffe blocked his shot!
But that didn't keep Ted from trying
and he scored quite a lot.

The whole crowd was nervous about the close game,
they were on the edge of their seat!
Will Ted become the winner or will it sadly end in defeat?

It was down to the last point
and the score was tied,
When Ted stole the ball from Barry the Bull
and he ran down the side.

Ted took the last shot and
it fell right into the hoop!
And the whole crowd cheered, Sasha,
Frank, and the rest of the group.

Barry the Bull and Gabby the Giraffe were in shock, the never lost before!
And Ted now had basketball skills that no one could ignore.

"Congratulations, Ted" Barry the Bull walked over to Ted to say,
"Yeah!" added Gabby the Giraffe, "You really played great today!"

They learned a great lesson that day,
that anyone can become great at anything, even a sport,
It doesn't matter if you are big, two-legged or short.

All that matters is how much practice
you have and the dedication you show,
Because the more that you practice something
the more that you'll know.

Ted was thankful for his mom and
inspired by the words that she said,
From then on, he remembered to never give up,
and to always practice hard instead.

He made many new friends through basketball and was having fun as well,
And surely enough, Ted the tortoise was slowly coming out of his shell.

The End

About the Author

Alli and Adam Clay live in the sunny state of Arizona.
As mental health advocates and parents of four wonderful children,
it is their ultimate mission to guide children in a fun positive direction
and hope that their children's books can be the tool that does just that.
Their inspiration comes from their children, personal experiences
and understanding that there are joyful lessons
even in everyday struggles.

Made in United States
Orlando, FL
27 November 2021

10822233R00027